BANANA-BED 5000

BED-SWING 5000

NO MORE BEDTIME!

Chuck Richards

Crown Books for Young Readers
New York

Elliot was finally ready to try out his latest invention, the
FLING-SHOT 5000. Elliot would make sure to hit his target.
His sister, Abby, would hit her target, too.

"*READY . . . AIM . . .*"

"Abby and Elliot, it's time to come in and get ready for bed."

"But, Mom," pleaded Elliot.

"No 'ifs,' 'ands,' or 'buts' *about it*, kiddo. It's *time for bed!*"

Elliot didn't like bedtime at all. It always came before he was finished with his day.

And bedtime was an ongoing battle between Elliot and his parents, so he was constantly inventing new ways to stay up late.

Once Elliot duct-taped all his books together to make the **MEGA-BOOK 5000**, a bedtime story that would never end.

And then he came up with the **PILLOW-COPTER 5000**. Elliot had fun watching his parents try to catch *that* invention.

But Abby spoiled everything when she caught Elliot turning back the clock with the *TIME-SHIFTER 5000*.

Mom and Dad had finally had enough.

"You know better than to try something sneaky like this, young man."

"But *why* can't I stay up late?" begged Elliot.

Dad's answer was short and simple.

"Because at the end of the day, son, it's time to go to bed."

For his punishment, Elliot would have to go to bed an hour earlier for a whole week.

But Elliot couldn't sleep. His head was full of ideas.

"If it's time to go to bed at the end of the day, then a day that never ends is exactly what I need," he grumbled.

At school the next day, the librarian, Mr. Takaki, helped Elliot find out more about how day turned into night.

Elliot read about how Earth and seven other planets orbit around the sun.

He also learned that Earth spins like a top.

Mr. Takaki explained, "As the Earth spins, we face toward the sun during the day, and away from it at night."

It all seemed so simple.

And then, suddenly, it dawned on Elliot. If he could build a machine to stop Earth from spinning, the day would never end. And that meant . . . NO MORE BEDTIME!

Elliot raced home after school
and turned the garage into his
laboratory. Here he would design
his top-secret machine.

He began with drawings and
models of different ideas and
tested each one out.

Elliot found parts for his invention wherever he could.
He discovered lots of good stuff on trash day . . .

. . . and he brought home some other things he needed from
Dizzy Daisy's Junkyard.

The machine was finally ready! Elliot took over
the entire toolshed for his creation.

The **SUN-SNAGGER 5000** sprouted up over the rooftops! Elliot decided to wait until Saturday to activate it. After all, why waste all this on a never-ending school day?

As soon as the sun reached the perfect place in the sky, Elliot flipped the switch. He felt the Earth *RUMBLE* and *LURCH* until it came to a complete stop.

The *SUN-SNAGGER 5000* worked!

Elliot's friends were so excited about never having to go to
school again that they celebrated with an *ELLIOT DAY* parade!
All the kids began to live like there was no tomorrow.

They had a gigantic water balloon fight. Elliot cranked up
his ***BALLOON-SLINGER 5000*** and soaked everyone.

Then Elliot invented the *TURBO-SWING 5000* and all the kids took it for a spin.

And when Elliot introduced the **BOUNCY-BOOT 5000**, even games like hopscotch and leapfrog became new and exciting.

Playing in the hot sun was making everyone thirsty. When Abby set up a lemonade stand, she couldn't make drinks fast enough . . . until Elliot built the **LEMON-AIDER 5000**.

But as the day wore on and on, Elliot began to realize that there were some drawbacks to making time stand still.

Sure, all the old people (like his parents) were happy because they would never get any older.

But this also meant that Elliot would never get any older, either. He would never get his driver's license. He would never grow up.

Elliot's birthday would have been next month. Elliot loved his birthday parties. Too bad today wasn't his birthday.

Elliot also realized there would never be any other holidays . . .

. . . no more Fourth of July . . .

. . . no more Halloween . . .

. . . no more Thanksgiving . . .

. . . and, worst of all, no more Christmas!

Elliot was also beginning to feel very, very sleepy.
He finally had to admit that today had been *too* long.

He decided the time had come to switch off the *SUN-SNAGGER 5000*. Elliot could feel the Earth *LURCH* and *RUMBLE* as it started to spin again, and day turned slowly into night.

Someday Elliot would get his driver's license, after celebrating many, many birthdays. He would grow so old that nobody would ever tell him when to go to bed again.

But right now, it finally felt like it really *was* time to go to bed.

And although he didn't know it yet, Elliot was about to get the best night's sleep he'd ever had.

For my editor, Emily Easton, who always manages
to get a better book out of me than the one
I would have come up with by myself —C.R.

Visit us on the Web! rhcbooks.com
Educators and librarians, for a variety of teaching tools, visit us at RHTeachersLibrarians.com

Library of Congress Cataloging-in-Publication Data:
Names: Richards, Chuck, author, illustrator.
Title: No More Bedtime / Chuck Richards.
Description: First edition. | New York: Crown Books for Young Readers, [2019] | Summary: Young
inventor Elliot, frustrated by bedtime always stopping his fun, asks the school librarian
how day turns to night, then invents a way to stop Earth from spinning.
Identifiers: LCCN 2018056899 | ISBN 978-0-553-53561-7 (hc) | ISBN 978-0-553-53562-4 (glb) |
ISBN 978-0-553-53563-1 (epub)
Subjects: | CYAC: Bedtime—Fiction. | Inventors—Fiction. | Family life—Fiction.
Classification: LCC PZ7.R37858 No 2019 | DDC [E]—dc23

MANUFACTURED IN CHINA
10 9 8 7 6 5 4 3 2 1   First Edition

ROCK-A-BED 5000

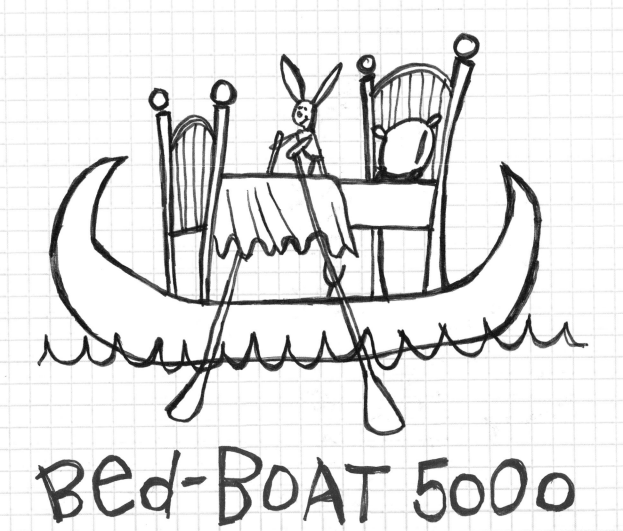

BED-BOAT 5000